MONSO

Dogs

ISBN : 978-1-80068-356-3

Written and Illustrated by Thurston Jones

A drop of rain
splashed onto Nuch's
nose;
For now, the
monsoon has started
to slow.

Chai paws for a home
that's barely afloat;
As Maya now shakes
a soggy, wet coat.

One favourite place
to start their day,
Is on a high roof of a
small cafe.

A breakfast call from
parrots up high;
As they eat all the
food that's left behind.

Beside empty tracks, along dusty roads;
Maya hopes a place will soon be called
home.
To keep her pups all happy and warm;
Before the rains of a coming storm.

It's tough to roam in a
monsoon flood,
So a boat is launched
from the slippy mud.

Chai tugs Nuch's ears to
help her twin;
As he paddles along
learning to swim.

Now, Maya remembers
being a pup,
With a feeling so warm
that she called it love.

And kindness in people
will one day win;
Along with some pennies
found in a tin.

A cool, damp forest is fun for dogs;
Whilst sniffing trunks and chasing frogs.
Up through the trees, so near the skies;
They sweetly howl with monkeys high.

Behind sandy dunes,
is a place to stay,
So Maya allows her
pups to play.

Both dig for toys and
catch soft balls;
And in the box, they
collect them all.

All clean and fresh from summer's rain;
Now curled in sands by splashing waves.

The ember of sun drifts them to sleep,
As it sinks beneath the ocean's deep.

For now, is the time when dreams are alive!
And from this soft night, a legend arrives.
Our friends, how they play as the boatman rows;
Then plunge in the blue to the waters below.

Whooshing through seas, the stream how it shines,
With coral and fish of different kinds.
An octopus waves as a turtle swims by;
A flash of sea sparkle when the manta ray glides.

And up from the deep, they race to the skies.

Chai, Nuch and Maya wag tails goodbye;

With one last, big blow from a fat whale's spout,
They shoot from the ocean to the stars all about.

A drop of rain splashed onto Nuch's nose.
The boatman has gone, as Maya is first
To open her eyes back on firm Earth;
But Chai's still asleep, twitching her toes.

MONSOON Dogs

Teaching kids about the environment is an important part of their education and also an important part of how they can make a difference today and in the future. Each picture below may be used to teach children about an environmental issue.

Page description	Environment issue
'A drop of rain'	Climate change
'One favourite place'	Food waste
'Along narrow tracks'	Displacement
'It's tough to roam'	Flooding/ water pollution
'Now, Maya remembers'	Population increase/ homelessness
'A cool, damp forest'	Deforestation
'Behind sandy dunes'	Plastic pollution
'All clean and fresh'	Global warming
'For now is the time'	Ocean acidification
'Whooshing through the seas'	Loss of biodiversity

Written and Illustrated by Thurston Jones

Dog Tales Series also includes Temple Dogs.

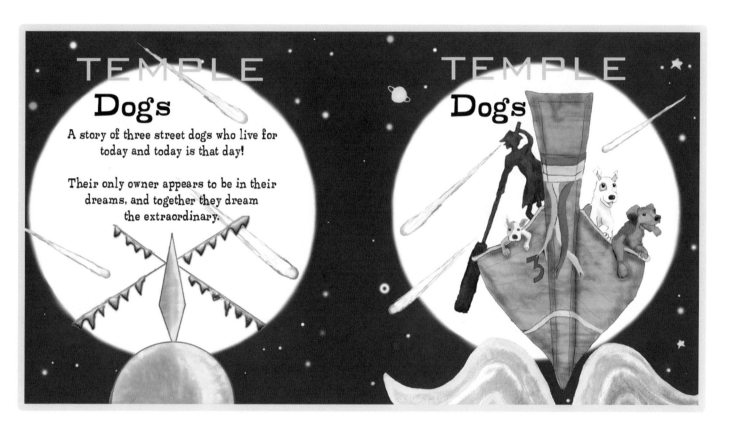

Printed in Poland
by Amazon Fulfillment
Poland Sp. z o.o., Wrocław

87818859R00018